Diamond in the Dirt 4

By Carde'l

Published by Stone Ink
Printed in the United States of America

Carde'ls contact info:
Email: cardelunlimited@gmail.com
Instagram: @Card_e_l
Facebook: CardelWrites and StoneInkPublication

CHAPTER 1

Benji was in his cell lying flat on his back in his bunk with his head resting on a pillow. To the officers and inmates walking pass his cell, it appeared as if he was just staring up at the ceiling but in all actuality the eyes in his mind was looking at something way more serious approaching him: The ultimate fight for his freedom. And it came closer and closer as the days passed by.

Benji made sure he was well prepared by studying his case religiously. Even though there were several loopholes in his case, he knew that if the eye witness got on the stand and testified it would be a wrap for him. He would be found guilty of all accounts. *Damn man, if I blow trial these crackers gonna roof me*, Benji said to himself. A feeling of depression came over him. He was in a very fucked up predicament with no one to call on to handle things for him. He hadn't heard from All Things since god knows when, and being under the impression that Real was dead and gone dimmed his bright light of hope a long time ago.

Benji finally snapped out of his caged thoughts when he heard the correctional officer outside of his cell in the day space shout out.

"Trays up!"

He climbed out of his bunk, put on his bright orange jumper and orange shoes and grabbed his spoon off the shelf before walking out of is cell. He strolled down the walkway behind the cage that led to the day space. A few inmates rushed pass him trying to hurry and get in line so they could grab their food. *As soon as one of these dumb ass lil niggas run into me I'm gonna break their face,* he said to himself getting aggravated. He tightly balled his fist while walking towards the long line of inmates waiting to get their meal.

Benji wasn't too much of a gun play type of guy, but when it came to jail scuffles he was vicious. Especially since he worked out during the majority of the years he was incarcerated, which gave him a very husky build. He just hated when in the mist of a brawl someone would try and grab his long dreads that grew all the way down to his back.

When Benji stepped in line, he had to wait a few seconds before it was his turn to grab his platter from the kitchen worker who wore an all white suit and gloves.
"What's going on big bro?" The worker greeted.
 "You already know man, same fight different round."

Benji walked away with his tray and grabbed a seat at a table all the way in the back of the unit near the shower area. He opened his platter and began eating his food. The several inmates sitting at the table near him were doing the same thing.

About 45 minutes later, Benji and a few other inmates from his neighborhood sat in the blue plastic chairs looking at the T.V. that hung on the wall underneath the metal stairwell.

"Damn her ass fat as hell," one of the young men stated excitedly while grabbing hold of his manhood.

His lustful eyes watched the thick yellow bone on the T.V. She wore a two piece bikini showing off her booty as it jiggled while she walked on the beach. Benji twisted his face up and took his eyes off the T.V. to look at the young man sitting beside him.

"Come on man, it ain't that serious. What you about to start whacking off live in the day space?"

The other young men sitting beside them began laughing.

"Nah bruh, she do gotta fat ass," one of the other young men said while chuckling.

"Man her ass ain't fat, the only reason it's shaking is because she's running," Benji shot back motioning his hands toward the T.V. "My main lady with all her clothes on turn me on more than that shit right there."

Suddenly, everyone on the unit quickly turned their heads when they heard the sally port door slowly open. They watched as two new inmates entered the unit holding their white pillow and blankets in one hand, and their picture card in the other. One of the new commitments was a white old guy with grey hair and the other one was a tall dark skin young fella.

Damn that look like my lil bruh a little bit, Benji thought to himself. He watched the two new inmates give their picture cards to the correctional officer sitting at the desk before focusing back on the T.V.

"You're in cell B-8," the officer told the new inmate.

The officer pointed to the cell and placed their picture cards in the picture book.

As Soon as Real turned around and started walking towards his cell he spotted Benji leaned back in his seat with his arms folded across his chest looking up at the T.V. *Check big bro out. Weight all up and shit!* Real said to himself grinning as he placed his blanket and pillow on one of the metal tables.

Real had sent Benji flicks and did everything else he was supposed to do, but never came to visit him just to be on the safe side knowing how the Feds and state operated. So in all actuality this was Real's very first time being in Benji's presence since the alphabet boys slammed the cuff's on him and snatched him from off the streets.
"What's good big bro!" Real greeted excitedly.

He walked up on the side of Benji. Benji turned his head along with the other men that sat around him. He looked up at Real with a puzzled look on his face. *Oh shit. This nigga think I'm dead*, Real thought. There was too much going on at once, it had slipped his mind that everyone in the city was under the impression that he was dead.

"It's me nigga, ya bro Real", he said looking Benji in the eyes.

Real had surpassed Benji's status in the streets and was now considered legendary, but he still respected and looked up to Benji since he was the one that introduced him to the game.

Benji's eyes grew wide and he quickly rose from his seat and hugged Real tight as if he was trying to squeeze the life out of him.

"Where the fuck you been at all this time? They said you was dead."

Benji tried his best to hold back the tears. After having it in his mind that Real was dead for so long, seeing him alive caused a lot of emotions to come over him and you could hear it all in his voice.

Real and Benji began conversing and showing each other love while majority of the people on the unit stopped what they were doing and focused in on the two. Most of the men knew who Real was and heard many stories about him, so they were very interested in hearing what the two had to say.

"Man it was too much shit going on, I had to get low," Real started to explain.

He looked around and noticed that everyone was watching.

"Let's go inside ya cell and talk cause these muhfuckas out here on some nosey shit."

Benji looked around and saw that Real was right. "Yeah, they on some other shit out here. Come on."

On his way back to his cell, Benji said to himself, *Watch when this nigga see this shit.* Once the two made it inside Benji's cell, Real closed the door and grabbed a seat on the metal stool while Benji sat on his bunk. "Yeah, but um like I was saying…Me and my baby mom, Wild Sal, and a few more of my soldiers was just in a wild shootout with ya boy Snake Eyes."

Benji was very much in tune with the streets so he already heard about Snake

Eyes murdering Real and taking over his empire.

"I got hit in the leg and went to the hospital to get fixed up and thats when the D.T's and Feds came there and snatched me up."

"Word up! The Feds too?"

"Hell yeah. That bitch ass nigga Snake Eyes thought I was dead after hitting me point blank range with the pump. So I hit up All Things and had him cut into his political connections to make it look like I really died. Right now I think they investigating the situation and trying to figure out what they're going to do with me. Damn man, I hope shit don't link back to All Things."

Real knew that if the Feds came and grabbed All Things too he wouldn't be able to avenge his father's death. *Should I tell this nigga about the situation with me and All Things?* Real asked himself. *Nah, that shit too personal, I'm gonna just keep it to myself.*

"So you mean to tell me All Things helped you fake your death?" Benji asked in amazement.

"Yeah."

"You niggas was out there on some real live T.V. shit huh."

"Yeah man, shit crazy right?"

"Yup, and it's about to get a whole lot crazier. Watch when you see this shit."

Benji grabbed a manilla envelope from under his mattress, pulled out a thick stack of papers, and began scanning through them.

"Damn man, where the shit at", he stated in a low tone. "Oh here it go."

He pulled out two sheets from the stack of papers, then handed them to Real.

"What's this?" Real asked.

"My discoveries. Go head and read it."

As Real read the papers his eyes grew wide and his mouth fell open in shock.

"Oh shit! You mean to tell me this nigga out here doing all this super gangster slime ball shit and he snitching!"

Real couldn't believe his eyes when he read the paper work on the only eye witness to Benji's case. Unbeknownst to the two, Snake Eyes was the confidential informant that set everything up in Benji's federal case. Benji copped out way before trial so he never got a chance to find out. Snake Eyes had it in his mind that once he sent Benji away he would be blessed with the plug to keep the ship moving on the streets. But to his surprise Benji gave it to Real instead. After that Snake Eyes became extremely envious and that's when he put his treacherous scheme into motion and smashed Real in to pieces with his poisonous black hand of betrayal.

Knowing that Benji didn't get the extensive length of time in the Feds he expected, and was on his way home in just a few years, Snake Eyes decided to wrap him up in a murder that he actually witnessed him commit with his own eyes to prevent him from coming home.

Seeing the surprised look on Real's face, Benji just shook his head.

"That nigga shot the fuck out ain't he?"

Real sighed out loud as he closed his eyes for a few seconds and then looked up at Benji.

"Damn man! This snake ass nigga was there when I caught a double murder and a whole lot of other shit. He probably the reason I'm charged too."

"I hate to say it man, but nine times out of ten that police ass nigga went in on you neph."

"I got to get the fuck out of here!" Real yelled angrily.

He balled his fist up and slammed it against the desk. After seeing what he just saw and hearing how those detectives were talking he ain't no how things were going to turn out.

During the remainder of the night the two continued to catch up on what was going on. Benji got a good look deep into Real's eyes and saw every bit of pain the ghetto had put him through. Benji knew that he was no longer the same young boy that was once captivated by the allure of the street life.

CHAPTER 2

A few weeks passed by and Snake Eyes still couldn't get over the fact that Real was really alive after all this time.Not only that, Dynasty who he was blindly infatuated with, had pretended to be his wifey just to set him up for the perfect kill. It's crazy because the sick bastard wasn't even that mad at Dynasty for doing what she did. He was more angry with Real for having complete control over something he wanted to possess so desperately.

After being robbed for all of his drugs and money, Snake Eyes didn't have any product to supply his die hard workers with, causing his empire to slowly crumble. Broke, desperate, and knowing Real and his crew was on his heels something serious, Snake Eyes laid low on the outskirts of Trenton along with his elite circle and began robbing banks in an attempt to accumulate enough money to purchase a large amount of cocaine and dope in order to save their empire before it was too late.

"Everybody get the fuck on the ground!" Snake Eyes yelled aggressively.

He and Low Down were masked up and dressed in all black when they rushed through the entrance glass doors, aiming their handguns at the people standing around in the bank. Everyone gasped and their eyes grew wide in fear. They quickly began doing exactly what they were commanded to do.

Low Down made his way to the center of the spacious lobby and began surveying the people on the floor with his gun drawn, making sure no one tried to play hero and save the day. Snake Eyes jumped on the counter and aimed his gun at the white female clerk's head.

"You press that fucking button and I'm gonna blow ya head off," he barked harshly.

The white lady gasped in fear for her life and she swiftly put her hands in the air.

"Now hurry up and fill this muhfucking bag up!" He demanded in a menacing tone.

Snake Eyes took a black book bag from off his back and handed it to the teller who was extremely nervous. She hurriedly unlocked the safe under the counter and began stuffing wads of cash inside the bag.

"Hurry the fuck up!"

Snake Eyes pressed the barrel of the gun forcefully against her head. Tears began pouring from her eyes and down her white cheeks.
"Please don't kill me," she cried shaking uncontrollably.

Once the teller filled the bag she handed it over to Snake Eyes who, in return, smacked her across the head with his pistol.

"Agghh!" She screamed in agony as she fell to the floor holding the bleeding gash in her head.

Snake Eyes jumped off the counter.
"Come on lets go!"

He and Low Down rushed towards the exit. As the two darted out of the bank and began running across the street, two police officers cruising in their patrol car spotted them.

"Tom you see that?" The short fat officer exclaimed excitedly without taking his eyes off the two masked men.

It was the officer's first day on duty so he was very eager to make his first bust.

"Yeah I see it Bill", his partner who was driving, responded sounding more nervous than anything while slowly driving towards the two.

"Well hurry up and drive before they get away," Bill urged looking at his partner like he was crazy.

Tom immediately turned the sirens on and slammed his black boot on the gas peddle. The patrol car sped up the street as the two masked men were running across it.

"Oh shit hurry up! Hurry up!"

Snake Eyes began to panic as he made his way to the getaway car. Low Down was right beside him. Bill climbed out of the patrol car.

"Freeze!" He yelled while aiming his gun at the two men.

BLOW! BLOW! Snake Eyes turned around and let off two shots, hitting the officer in the forehead. His hat flew off and his brains splattered all over the car. After seeing what just happened to his partner, Tommy became terrified and immediately dropped his weapon and dove back into the squad car ducking for cover. The masked men climbed into their getaway car, which was left running, and sped off recklessly.

CHAPTER 3

Pondering all the possibilities to his situation amongst other things, Real was sick to his stomach until he finally talked to his attorney and found out that some how the Feds investigation went sour. They couldn't do anything but recharge him with the double murder and release him on the enormous bail he was already out on. Real was now full of life and ready to get back out there to the streets.

Benji and Real were playing cards while the other inmates played board games.

"Hold up man, let me look around and make sure it ain't no witnesses out here", Real joked as he turned his neck to survey the crowd in the day space. "I just bodied me a nigga!"

Real slammed the red cards on the table.
"Lil nigga you ain't body me. I know I got at least one point in here,"Benji shot back as he scooped up his cards and began counting them.

They were playing a card game called Casino, best out of 5, and the score was 2 to 1 Benji's way. But being that a body counted as two wins it placed Real as the winner.
"Ain't no need to check the deck, all the money over here baby boy", Real said smiling as he placed all of his point cards on the table.
"Damn! You got that."

Benji grabbed all of the cards from off the table and began shuffling them. *Man I been playing this shit for almost 7 years behind the wall. I can't believe I let this lil nigga come fresh in the building and beat me,* Benji said to himself feeling a little salty. Even though it was just a game, Benji hated loosing no matter what it was.

"Lets run it back."

Real burst into a loud laughter, noticing the displeased look on his face. This was his first time ever winning a game against Benji throughout the several weeks they've been playing cards.

"Nah, I don't fee like running it back right now,"Real said in between laughs. "I'm trying to enjoy this win for at least a half hour."

He then grabbed the plastic cup of coffee, put it to his lips, and swallowed the last little bit that was left. Benji removed the two long dreads that were hanging down in front of his face and continued shuffling the cards.

"A half hour? Nigga they be done told you to pack ya bags by then. Didn't you say ya peoples was on they're way up here."

Knowing his loyal young gunner Real would take care of the snitch ass eye witness, Benji was just as happy for Real to get back on the streets.

"Yeah, you right. Let me go make us another cup of coffee real quick."

Real grabbed his empty plastic cup, got up from his seat, and made his way behind the gate. He went to Benji's cell to get the coffee and then back into the day space to heat it up in the microwave. Afterwards, Real sat back down at the table with Benji.

For the next hour the two laughed, joked, drunk back to back cups of coffee, and played as many rounds of Casino as they could. Then suddenly the phone on the C.O.'s desk began ringing. RING! RING! RING! RING! Benji scooped the ten of spade up with the ten of diamond and placed it in his stack of cards. He glanced at the short dark skin correctional officer, then looked at Real.

"That's probably ya ride right there."

Real threw his card on the table and looked up just as the officer hung up the phone.

"Mr. Johnson pack you baggage. Your ride is outside waiting for you."

"I told you," Benji said.

A smile slowly came across Benji's face and he placed the cards on the table. Everyone in the day space stopped what they were doing and turned to look at Real as he got up from his seat.

"Let me go grab my shit", he said trying to control his excitement.

Real rushed behind the cage towards the cell. Within seconds, he was eagerly making his way back through the day space towards the officer's desk holding his pillow and blanket.

Benji turned and stood up from the metal stool as Real approached him. "Alright lil bro, you be safe out there."

The two slapped hands and embraced each other. Benji knew Real had touched more paper than he ever thought about having and was very proud of him. He felt as though he played a major part of Real becoming the young legend he was today.

"You already know! You just make sure you hold ya head up," Real responded.

He paused for a few seconds and stared deep into Benji's eyes. Benji never showed any signs of stress during the time the two spent together, but there were certain moments when Real could see the worried look in his eyes, and this was one of those times. "Don't worry, I'm going to take care of everything", he assured seriously.

Benji slowly nodded his head, knowing Real to always be true to his word.

"Alright Mr. Johnson, your escort is here," the male officer said impatiently.

A light skin female escort officer walked through the sally port and onto the unit. The male officer pulled Real's picture card from out the picture book.

"Much love big bro," Real said.

He turned around, grabbed his picture card, and made his way towards the sally port. Benji stood a few feet away watching Real walk behind his escort. The metal bar door began to slowly close.

"Don't forget to check up on my girl and make sure she alright for me!"

Benji grew kind of suspicious as far as the love of his life China Doll was concerned. Ever since his feet touched the county jail she been missing visits, not picking up the phone at times when he called, and wasn't responding to his letters as quick as she used to.

The few times Benji brought China Doll's name up, Real wanted to tell him so badly about the scandalous stunt she pulled the last time he stopped by the house. He knew that Benji damn near loved her more than he loved himself, and not knowing how he would react, Real decided to keep it silent which bothered him. Real didn't want to stop by her house but because he sensed that Benji was stressed out over China Doll he told himself that he would do him the favor.

The sally port exit door opened and Real and the escort stepped in to the hallway. When Real finally got to the large parking lot he saw Dynasty. She was wearing a purple and gray Fendi jacket with her hair in a sleek long ponytail looking sexy as fuck. She was sitting on the hood of a burgundy F150 pickup truck that was parked near the guard booth. As Real approached she slid off and dove on him with open arms.

"Baby I missed you so much!"

Dynasty hugged her man tight. Real closed his eyes and slowly breathed heavily out of his nose in relief. "That was a close one. I thought they was about to sit me down for the long ride."

He kissed Dynasty on the forehead.
"Me too", Dynasty said looking Real in the face. "Thank God they didn't. Now lets hurry up and get to your sister's spot. She miss you like crazy and your daughter do too."
"Why she ain't ride up here with you then?"
"Because I told her we needed some time alone before we made it to the house."

Dynasty had a seductively naughty grin on her face.

"Now come on."

Real smirked knowing exactly what his lady's freaky little mind was thinking about as she turned around and sexily strutted towards the passenger side of the vehicle.

"Where Wild Sal at," he asked while opening the car door.

Dynasty proceeded to get in the car without answering him. Assuming that she didn't hear him, Real asked again.

"Where Sal at?"

Dynasty breathed heavily from her nose and she shook her head. *I'm trying to bust a quick nut and this nigga worried about some damn Sal*, she thought to herself with an attitude.

"He at ya sister house waiting for you like everybody else," she responded sarcastically rolling her eyes at him.

Real began looking around and surveyed the area for a few seconds, knowing Wild Sal wouldn't let her take the trip to come pick him up alone.

Snake Eyes and Low Down sat on opposite sides of the king size bed with their backs to one another. They were posted up in a five star hotel room out in Langhorne, Pennsylvania counting all of the money they accumulated from the several bank robberies they and their team of wild young boys committed. "Damn bruh, I just counted two hundred grand and it still look like I got at least fifty more to count up", Low Down said excitedly.

He was wrapping a rubber band around a wad of cash.
"Let me count it and see exactly what it is."

Low Down reached down and grabbed the fifth of Hennessy that was near his foot on the floor. He took a quick swig and sat the bottle back down. He started back counting the rest of the cash from inside the black duffle bag sitting in between his legs.
"Shit, I wasn't too far from it. It's 45k bruh."

Low Down shifted his body to look at Snake Eyes. All he saw was the barrel of a black .50 caliber handgun. "What da…!"

BOOM! Snake Eyes shot Low Down right in between the eyes, causing his brains to splatter out the back of his head and all over the white wall and wooden dresser. He then got up, stuffed the wads of cash inside of two duffle bags, and rushed out the door leaving his right hand man's lifeless body sprawled out on the floor near the bathroom door.

After being desperately broke and finally getting his hands on a nice amount of change, greed took over his already polluted mind causing him to murder the only man in the world that truly had his best interest at heart.

Snake Eyes already told himself that he was going to rob a few more banks, then steal all of the money that his young boys accumulated from their bank robberies and flee the town and start a new drug empire some where new.

Real and Dynasty couldn't wait to fulfill each other's sexual appetite. As soon as they stepped inside the hotel room and closed the door, they immediately began kissing each other like hot and horny wild beasts while roughly pulling one another's clothes off before falling onto the king size bed.

"Give me my dick," Dynasty demanded as she crawled on all fours in between Real's long chocolate legs, grabbing hold of his dick.

She took his thick pole in to her mouth and began sucking on it for dear life. The feeling of Dynasty's warm tongue caused Real's body to immediately tense up as he let out a low grunt. He used his elbow to support him and he slightly sat up. He began to gently rub on the back of her neck and right shoulder looking down at her go to work.

Staring directly into Real's eyes, Dynasty's huge pink lips sucked hungrily on his long rod slurping loudly while quickly moving her head up and down and in a circular motion. Thick globs of saliva began slowly pouring down his balls. The feeling caused Real to quickly tighten up his toned butt cheeks. With her free hand

Dynasty began rubbing on Reals's rock hard abs and chiseled chest. The intense eye to eye contact and the sexy facial expression Real continuously made in pleasure immediately caused her clitoris to swell up and throb intensely. She was so turned on that sweet juices from her warm honey pot began slowly easing down her huge inner thighs. Dynasty wanted Real to dig her guts out so bad she din't care about him returning the favor. She removed her lips from his penis and began stroking it with her hand.

"This my big dick right daddy?"

She knew Real loved whenever she got possessive over him.

"Yeah," he moaned in between low grunts looking down at Dynasty slowly twirling her long pink tongue around the head of his penis.

"Well give it to me then."

She rolled over and laid on her back, spreading her toned legs. Completely aroused, Real immediately climbed out of the bed, turned around, and stood by the edge. He then reached his arm out and tightly grabbed Dynasty by her ankles and pulled her towards him. "This what you want," he said as he grabbed his manhood.

He slowly slid inside of her wetness and began stroking her slowly but deeply.

"Ummm," she moaned.

Dynasty's body tensed up for a few seconds from the feeling of her baby daddy's stiffness stretching her insides. While Real held on to one ankle, Dynasty grabbed her other leg and pulled it back towards her head as far as she could allowing Real to dig deeper inside of her honey pot. He felt Dynasty's juice box getting wetter and wetter.

Every stroke Real took caused him to throw his head back. He fought to keep his lustful heavy eyes open in order to focus in on the erotic facial expressions Dynasty made. He picked up his thrusting pace and lowered his head and began sucking on her toes, licking on the bottom of her small foot. A tingling sensation traveled through Dynasty's body, driving her wild. She immediately placed two fingers on her swollen clitoris and began rubbing it fiercely.

"Oooohh...It feel like I'm about to cum", she moaned.

Her lips quivered as her lazy eyes watched Real's hard rod go in and out, in and out. The pleasant sight of every muscle in Real's upper body flexing as he stroked her deeply, powerful, and fast caused her to cum instantly.

"Awwww, I'm cumming!"

Her eyes rolled behind her head and her toes curled up in Real's mouth. The thick creamy cum slowly oozed from her slit onto his shaft. Dynasty removed her fingers from her wet pussy and put them in her mouth and began licking on them seductively. Real felt like he was about to explode. He grabbed hold to one of her titties, squeezing it tightly. He began fucking her like he was a mad man. Seeing how excited Real became she knew he was about to cum any second.

"Yes daddy…give it to me!"

She caressed the lower part of Real's chest. His grunts began echoing throughout the room. All it took was the feeling of Dynasty's soft hands on Real's skin to turn his moment of ecstasy into an overwhelming climax. His jaws clenched as his body stiffened. "Aaagghh!" He roared in pleasure as thick globs of semen erupted out of his throbbing penis into Dynasty's wetness.

He grew weak in the knees and immediately caught himself before falling on top of her.

CHAPTER 4

Real and Dynasty walked through the door and saw his sister and Kim sitting beside one another on the long cream leather couch in front of the T.V. He looked down and noticed his shirtless daughter in the middle of the living room playing with her toys. "There go daddy Zah Zah!" Tadasia said while smiling and motioning both of her hands towards Real before standing up from the couch.

Zanyah quickly turned her head and her eyes lit up at the sight of her father. She dropped her toys, got up on her feet and rushed towards her dad with open arms.
"Daddy!" She shouted joyfully.

Real couldn't help but smile at his daughter's excitement as he leaned down to scoop her up. He gave her a big kiss on her soft cheeks.

"What's up lil mamma you miss me?"

"I miss you", Zanyah was able to say the words correctly as she rubbed on Real's face.

"Yes she did miss her dad. That's all she was talking about, ain't that right Zah Zah," Tadasia said in a soft tone smiling as she strolled across the living room and stood directly in front of her little brother.

She went to give her niece a kiss on the cheek, but to her surprise Zanyah quickly turned her face away.

"I know her little two-faced behind ain't acting funny because her dad here," Tadasia said.

Real, Dynasty, and Kim all started laughing.

"That little girl is too much," Dynasty said in between laughs. She stood close beside Real shaking her head.

"It's alright though, when it's time for me to eat my cookies and cream ice cream I'm gonna act funny too."

Tadasia began moving her neck from side to side while talking and rolling her eyes at her niece.

"What's up big sis, I heard you missed me too."

Real hugged his big sister before with his free hand and gave her a kiss on the cheek. Zanyah was trying to push her aunt away from Real.

"My daddy!"

"This little girl is really showing out," Tadasia said.

She looked at her niece and then back at Real.

"I know you ready to eat a good home cooked meal after eating that bull crap they feed you in jail. I made a big dinner for you," she stated as she turned around to go back in to the kitchen.

"Where Uncle Sal and J.J. at?" Real asked Kim.

"I don't know, they left right behind Dynasty when she went to go pick you up."

"Oh yeah."

Real knew that Wild Sal followed them and was still some where in the area.

"I don't know why you still standing up like you're a guest or something. Come over here and have a seat," Kim said as she patted on the cushion.

Real and Dynasty walked towards the couch. Kim stood up to give Real a big hug.

"It feels good to be home with your family don't it?" "No no no. My daddy," Zanyah was still trying to push everyone away from her dad.

"You acting funny with ya grandmom too Zah Zah," Kim said while laughing.

Kim, Real, and Dynasty were all talking for a few minutes when Tadasia walked back in to the living room with a plate of food in her hand.

"Here little brother I made your favorite. Go ahead and stuff your face."

She handed him a plate of baked macaroni and cheese, boneless fried chicken drenched in hot sauce, sweet corn, and homemade cheese mashed potatoes. Real's mouth began to water at the sight of the delicious looking meal.

"Dynasty hold Zah Zah for me while I eat."

As soon as Dynasty took Zanyah she began to cry and struggled to break loose from her mother.

"Girl if you don't calm ya little butt down, he ain't going no where."

"That little girl don't discriminate. She'll trade on the whole world for her dad," Tadasia chuckled.

Without waisting any time, Real started digging in his plate relentlessly. Knowing that he was going to be released from jail today, Real made sure he didn't eat any county meals for a whole day and a half so he could have an enormous appetite by the time he got home. Kim turned to look at Real.

"Dag on it boy, that food ain't gonna run off the plate. Slow down."

Real stopped eating for moment to look at Kim, grinning at her with a mouth full of food. He then began digging back into his plate. Within minutes, he finished his meal and sent his sister to make him seconds which he also quickly scarfed down.

Feeling like his stomach was about to burst, Real was now joyfully playing with his daughter on the couch while Kim, Dynasty, and Tadasia were talking loudly and watching father and daughter have a ball with each other. Real smiled as he lifted his daughter in the air looking into her wide eyes. He lowered her back down to his face and began blowing on her stomach, causing her to laugh uncontrollably.

Zanyah was having so much fun, she began moving and twisting wildly while her father held her. Suddenly she slipped from his grasp and began falling backwards. Real was able to catch her fall right before her head hit the ground.

"That was a close one!"

"Um hum, that's enough playing. Sit her little wild behind down," Dynasty said, feeling relieved that Real caught Zah Zah.

Zanyah smiled at her mother and continued to bounce around with her dad.

"I said play time is over, now sit ya little ass still!"

Dynasty swiftly snatched her from Real and sat her down on her lap. Zanyah began crying and extended her arms trying to go back to Real. Real tried to grab her but Dynasty moved his hand away.

"Ain't nothing. Her little ass gonna learn how to listen when I tell her to do something."

Dynasty loved her daughter and spoiled her rotten, but she still tried her best to put her foot down when she felt it was necessary. She made sure her little princess clearly understood who ran the show. Real hated to see his daughter cry.

"Come on baby, she ain't see me in a minute. Let her live. I'm not gonna throw her in the air anymore. We just gonna chill."

"Please just give her back to her dad so she could be quiet," Kim pleaded, frustrated with her daughter.

Dynasty balled her face up and smacked her teeth. "That's why she the way she is now."

She reluctantly handed her back to Real.

"Daddy got you now, everything gonna be alright", Real said as his daughter buried her face in his chest.

He started gently rubbing her on the back. Tadasia bust into laughter.
"That little girl is spoiled rotten."
"Tell me about it. Every time I try to put her in check he always coming to her rescue. She gonna grow up thinking she can get away with whatever she want", Dynasty said as she folded her arms across her chest.

"Shhh, I think she about to go to sleep", Real said in a low tone.

"It's about time, she been up since 6 in the morning," Kim chimed in.

"As soon as she fall asleep I'm gonna make a quick run down to my lawyer's office and grab my discoveries," Real said.

His attorney received the information a week ago but didn't want to send them to him while in the county jail to avoid the risk of someone stealing them out of his cell.

"Why y'all ain't go before y'all came here? You know that baby gonna go crazy if she wake up and you not here", Kim said.

"Oh shit, I knew I forgot to tell you something. Your discoveries are upstairs in my room. Your lawyer sent them the other day," Tadasia said.

Just as she stood up, Kim volunteered. "You don't have to get up, I'm about to go upstairs anyway. Where are they?" "It's on the dresser next to my bed in a brown envelope."

Kim made her way up the steps and leisurely strolled down the hallway until she got to Tadasia's room. She walked in the spacious bedroom and grabbed the big brown envelope, but was shocked when she noticed something else on Tadasia's dresser. *Oh my gosh, that's why he looked so familiar when I first met him,* Kim thought to herself.

Kim was staring at a large picture of Big Real and Nayla smiling and holding each other's hand. Kim went by the name T.T. back in the day and was the same female that was pregnant by Big Real and was with him the day he was murdered. After finding out she wasn't the only female pregnant by Big Real, she packed her belongings and moved down south and told herself never again. *How am I going to tell Real and Dynasty,* she thought. Kim just stood there for several seconds in a daze as she replayed the day Big Real was murdered. She finally made her way back downstairs.

Real saw Kim walking towards him so he handed the baby over to Dynasty. He noticed a very strange look on her face as she handed him the papers.

"Thanks, you alright?"

"Yeah baby, I'm good."

Kim sounded uneasy as she quickly looked down at the floor trying to avoid eye contact. Real raised a curious eyebrow as he tried to get a read on her. Dynasty noticed her mother's uneasiness too.

"Mom, you sure you alright?"

"Yeah, I'm good girl. I'm about to make a quick run to the store. I'll be right back."

Kim picked up her purse from off the couch and hurriedly walked out the door. Once the front door slammed shut everyone began looking at one another with puzzled looks on their faces.

"She looked like she saw a ghost upstairs or something," Tadasia said breaking the silence.

"Omar up there?" Real asked.

"No, he downstairs in the basement."

Real didn't know what to say or what to think so he left it alone and went back to the information in the manilla envelope. Real began reading the first few pages, but there really wasn't too much information. He wanted to get straight to the point, he began quickly scanning though the papers, eager to see exactly how much evidence they had on him. *Where is it at? Where is it?* He said to himself, continuously flicking through the pages. And then finally he found it.

"Yeah, this it right here."

THE SOLE EVIDENCE IN WHICH THE STATE OF NEW JERSEY HAS AGAINST MR. REAL JOHNSON IS AN EYE WITNESS, MR. SHAWN MCCRAY, PLACING HIM ON THE CRIME SCENE AS THE SHOOTER WHO MURDERED DONTE BROWN AND RAYSHAWN MYERS.

"I knew it!" Real exclaimed as he looked up at his baby mother.

After reading Benji's paperwork, he already had a feeling that Snake Eyes stool pigeon ass went in on him, but he was now actually reading it with his own eyes.

"You knew what?" Dynasty asked.
"This bitch ass nigga was the one that went in on me."

He held the paper up to Dynasty's face so she could read it. Real then turned his head when he noticed Omar walk into the living room.

"What's good Real. Back at 'em again huh", Omar greeted giving him a head nod.

"Yeah you know man, they can't hold a good nigga down for too long," Real responded charismatically as if nothing was bothering him.

Damn, where did Dynasty's mom go that fast? Fuck it, I'm going to do it anyway, Omar said to himself. He walked to where Tadasia was sitting and stood directly in front of her with a sexy smirk on his face looking down in to her eyes. He had his back turned to Real and Dynasty.

"Baby, will you marry me?"

Omar dropped down to one knee and pulled a small black suede box out of his pants pocket. He opened it, revealing a huge diamond ring. Tadasia was caught by surprise and gasped putting both hands over her mouth. She glanced at Real and Dynasty, who both were flabbergasted, waiting for her response.

CHAPTER 5

It was a little after 12 o'clock in the afternoon. Dark grey clouds slowly moved across the sky. Light drizzle hit the windshield as Real pulled inside the huge cemetery and slowly drove up the steep hill, parking his black F-150 underneath a huge tree. He pulled his black hoodie over his head and took a huge gulp from the clear bottle of Hennessy he held in his hand. "Ughh," he grunted as the burning sensation traveled down his chest.

He then climbed out of the truck and began walking through the field, headed towards his mother's and Kamikaze's grave. This would be the first time he payed the two a visit since the days of their funerals. He wished he could've came through more often but because of the way things went down back to back right after their deaths he was unable to.

When Real got closer to where they were buried he spotted their plots, causing all kinds of mixed emotions to overwhelm him. Every step he took towards his deceased loved ones, the more of what he felt deep in his heart increased.

Real approached the headstones and stopped dead in his tracks. Swallowing hard and tightening up his face, Real stared down at the huge picture of his mother that was engraved in her headstone. He then turned to look a Kaze's picture for a few seconds. Kaze had his hair in box braids dressed in all black looking like a straight up menace.

Real took notice to the well manicured grass, trying to look away in an attempt to keep his composure. He was hurting bad inside, more than ever. Real had Snake Eyes' slime ball piece of shit ass right in the palm of his hands, thanks to his clever baby mom, but let him slip away. Knowing he probably would never receive an opportunity like that again, a feeling of deep depression came over him whenever he thought about it. It didn't cause him to give up on himself though, he desperately told himself that no matter where he had to go, whatever he had to do, or when he had to do it, he was going to find his despicable enemy and make him suffer severely before destroying him completely. He knew it was either that or take the risk of Snake Eyes testifying against him during trial and spending forever and a day in prison. "Damn man, why everything keep turning up side down on me", Real said as he glanced up at the sky.

Real stepped closer to his mother's grave where he leaned down to sit on the wet grass. A tear slowly fell as a slight smirk crept across his face.

"What's up mom. Long time no hear from right? I miss you like crazy. I hope you not upset with me. I would've been stopped by more often but my whole life fell into a roller coaster ride ever since you passed away. I had to get low and move down south to get myself and several other things in order."

He paused for a few seconds before he continued.

"I found that light skin dude K.O. that hit you in the head with that heavy board in front of me when I was a kid. I know you remember because I didn't forget about it. Well I'm not going to go in to detail about how bad i did him, but just know he payed for it with the price of his life."

Relief and accomplishment came over Real as a flashback of doing K.O. dirty appeared in his mind. Suddenly the image of Snake Eyes' hideous face flashed in the back of his head.

"Just how that snake ass nigga gonna pay when I catch 'em again."

Tears began to pour down his chocolate cheeks.

"I promise", he assured as his voice cracked.

The determination in Real's voice could also be heard. Even though Real knew Snake Eyes was behind his mother's death, he still felt some type of way towards himself knowing he was the man that put the heroin on the streets.

"Well mom, I'll be back to visit you after I finish handling my handle."

Real stood up on his feet and wiped the back of his jeans off. He leaned down and kissed the picture of his mother's beautiful face.

"I love you."

Real stepped towards his right hand man's headstone. He wiped the tears from his face with the sleeve of his hoody, knowing the last thing Kaze would have wanted was for Real to be shedding tears on some mushy shit. He hurried up and got himself together.
"Damn man, I hope you ain't disappointed in me."

Real knew his right hand man would've brought drama in the worse way imaginable with nothing to talk about. He told himself he was going to keep his words short and simple, then go hunt down his prey like a starving lion lurking in a safari.

Real poured what was left of his bottle of Hennessy in the grass, and leaned down to sit the bottle close by Kaze's stone.

"Don't worry about nothing bro. I'm gonna get that nigga. I don't care if it's the last thing I do."

Real stormed off through the field, climbed in his truck and sped off. Hoping that his mother and Kaze wasn't turning over in their graves.

Real slowly drove down the long one way street China Doll lived on until he finally found a parking spot. He decided to bring Dynasty along with him just in case China Doll tried the same stunt she pulled the last time he stopped.

"Baby come on", he demanded as he took the key out the ignition.

The two got out of the car and began walking down the quiet street side by side.
"Damn baby, it look like it's about to rain again", Dynasty said as she looked up at the cloudy sky.

She began walking a little faster.

"Yeah, it do", Real agreed.

He put some pep in his step as well, trying to keep up with Dynasty.

Once the two made it on China's front porch, Real began knocking on the front door. KNOCK! KNOCK! KNOCK! He waited for a response for several seconds but didn't get one. *Damn I hope she still here*, he thought as he glanced at Dynasty.

"What you ain't call to make sure she was home before you came?"
"Nah. Benji asked me to pop up on her cause he ain't heard from her in a while. He getting kind of suspicious," Real explained in a low tone.
"Oh."

Real began knocking again, harder this time. KNOCK! KNOCK! KNOCK! Within seconds they heard footsteps running towards the door.
"Who is it?" China Doll asked in a high tone.
"It's Real."
China Doll opened the door and saw Real standing before her.

"Oh my gosh. I thought you were dead!" China Doll revealed looking both confused and surprised.

Real smirked.
"Nah, It was just a real big misunderstanding."

Everyone just stood there for a few seconds before Real spoke again.
"Ain't you gonna invite us inside."

China was so shocked to see him, she didn't even take notice to the strikingly beautiful red headed green eyed yellow bone standing a few feet away. *This must be his girl,* she thought as she looked at Dynasty and became jealous.

Not only was Dynasty just as sexy as China Doll, but Dynasty had someone

China Doll threw herself at but couldn't get.

"Oh yea, y'all come in. I was kind of lost for words," she admitted.

After Real and Dynasty stepped inside the house, China Doll closed the door behind them and then turned around. "Umm Real who's your little friend? I don't remember seeing her."

China Doll stood near her white suede couch that matched the entire living room set. She was dressed in a tight white v-neck short sleeve shirt. Her curly long hair was in a pony tail. China Doll had moved on with her life and started doing her own thing, basically turning her back on Benji the man that loved her and showed her through his actions during their entire relationship.

If you don't knock it off, Real thought.
"I could've sworn you met her before. Her name Dynasty, she my baby mom."

Baby mom huh, China thought.
"Awe, that's so cute. How you doing Dynasty, my name is China Doll."

Dynasty wasn't no slow chick, and immediately felt a negative vibe coming from the woman. She squinted her eyes as her intuition started kicking in.
"Nice to meet you."

An awkward silence filled the air for a few seconds before Real spoke again.

"So what's up with you and my brother Benji."

China Doll rolled her eyes at Dynasty before looking at Real.
"Ain't too much been up with me and Benji lately. I've been real busy you know."

China turned around and sat down on the couch and crossed her legs.
"Y'all two can grab a seat if y'all want."
"Nah that's alright, we won't be staying that long", Dynasty said.

China Doll chuckled, knowing she was getting under Dynasty's skin.
"Alright, that's fine…"

Before China Doll could finish her sentence, Real cut in.

"So damn, you've been up to go see him and see how he's doing? You know he about to start trial, he need as much support as he can get."

Real could see clearly that she gave up on Benji.

"Oh yeah, he about to start trial?"

China Doll was shocked. She didn't know much about law, but she did know that when someone went to trial they either come straight home or go straight to prison for a long time. The last thing she wanted to happen was for Benji to come home, get his paper back up, and act as if she never existed.

Real's eyes began to discretely scan the living room for any inklings of another man living in the house with her. Suddenly, he noticed a black pair of Stacy Adam's on the side of the white lazy boy chair near the fish tank. *Oh yeah, she got somebody living here with her*, he thought. China spoke up when she noticed Real's prying eyes.

"Yeah, you know what...I've been slipping lately. I guess it's just because he's been locked up for so long. It felt like he was never coming home sometimes. But now it's definitely time for me to get back on my shit. I'ma go up there to see him this week."

"Yeah, that's what you need to do. My big bro up there stressing and he need you right now."

"Don't worry, I'm gonna be up there first thing Saturday morning."

"When I talk to him I'll let him know."

Real and Dynasty began to make their exit out of the house. *She probably just talking*, Real thought.

"Alright, see y'all later," China Doll said in a sweet tone as she waved her hand still trying to dig deep under Dynasty's skin.

Real and Dynasty walked out the front door and closed it behind them. As soon as they stepped off the porch and were a few houses away, Dynasty cut in front her her baby dad, stopping him dead in his tracks.
"Now what the fuck was that about!"

Dynasty stood there with her hand on her hip. Real knew this was coming, and he didn't want to hide anything from his baby mom so he decided to tell the truth. He breathed heavily out of his nose and looked her dead in the eyes.

"A few years ago when Benji got bagged by the feds, she threw herself at me on some sleezy shit, but I denied her. This her first time seeing me since then, so I guess she on some other type of shit. That's why I brought you over here with me, cause I ain't beat."

"Did you tell Benji?"

"Nah, I ain't tell him because I didn't know how he was going to take it. Plus I didn't want him to be stressed out over her scandalous ass, he's deeply in love with her."

"Oh. That makes sense," Dynasty stated feeling relieved. "That bitch better fall back with all that sarcastic shit. She lucky I ain't smack the shit out of her ass."

CHAPTER 6

Snake Eyes was shirtless, exposing his skinny upper frame inside his single cell laying in the bunk wide awoke with his eyes closed trying to figure out how in the hell he was going to get himself out of the fucked up situation he was in. He was still the eye witness in Real's cases and hoped he could use that as leverage to get his bail lowered into a reasonable price. If that plan didn't fall through, he was thinking about giving his young soldiers up. The judge set his bail at 1 million dollars, which was too high for him to pay after being robbed for damn near everything he had. *Damn man, what the fuck was I thinking when I killed Low-Down.* Snake Eyes knew that Low-Down would've gotten the money up for him to post bail by any means necessary.

When Snake Eyes got locked up he was put in population on maximum security with a whole bunch of dudes he did mad dirt to on the street. They ended up jumping on Snake Eyes' ass, damn near beating him to death. After the fight, the administration put a special hold on him and housed him on a lock down unit. Snake Eyes didn't have any direct contact with anyone and only came out of his cell for an hour a day.

Snake Eyes heard someone tapping on his door.
"The nurse is here to see you, make sure you're dressed before you come to

the door," a white male officer ordered in a deep tone.

Snake Eyes opened is eyes and sat up. He grabbed his orange shirt from the metal railing connected to his bed and got dressed. He then climbed out of bed, and moped to the door. The correctional officer stepped aside, allowing the nurse to hand Snake Eyes his HIV medicine. The brown skin elderly nurse lady dressed in a white jacket and blue pants stepped to the door, leaned down, and opened the food slot connected to the door. She dumped several different color pills inside his hand.

"Do you have any water? You have to take them now in front of me", she said in a soft tone.

Snake Eyes was about to speak but got cut off.

"Oh yeah, you're going to need some water for all those damn pills", the officer joked, chuckling as he recognized exactly what kind of pills they were. "Now leave that man alone, that's not funny," the nurse said as she closed the food port.

"Fuck you! You gay muhfucka", Snake Eyes snapped dramatically, causing the nurse to jump back. "That'sss why I fucked your wife!"

"Don't make me pop your door and come inside there and beat your skinny ass," the officer barked.

The noise caused several inmates to come to their cell door and look out to see what was going on.

"Come inssside, I dare ya bitch asss!" Snake Eyes yelled angrily.

He took a few steps back, preparing for the C.O. to pop the door open. The officer sighed out loud in frustration. He caught himself after thinking about having a physical altercation with Snake Eyes, and risk the chance of catching H.I.V. Snake Eyes recognized that the C.O. didn't want any drama.
"Oh, that'sss what I thought muhfucka."

He turned around, grabbed his plastic cup from the desk, and made his way to the sink to get himself some water. The nurse stood at the door watching as Snake Eyes tossed the pills in his mouth, then drunk the cup of water to wash it down. The nurse was able to step off. *Bitch asss C.O. mussst not know who the fuck I am,* he thought to himself. He sat his cup on the table and climbed back in his bunk.

"I got to get the fuck out of thisss ssshit hole," he grumbled.

Snake Eyes closed his eyes and dozed off. About an hour later, Snake Eyes' eyes popped open when he heard his cell door open.

"What the fuck," he grumbled in a low tone when he saw the male officer step halfway inside.

"Pack your baggage, your bail has been posted."

"What!" Snake Eyes exclaimed.

"Hurry and pack your shit, you're going home," the officer stated impatiently.

The officer turned around and made his way back to his desk. Snake Eyes anxiously climbed out of bed and put his orange jumper and skippies on. He then snatched his white sheets and pillow up and rushed out of his cell, leaving everything else behind. He grabbed his picture card from the C.O. at the desk and exited the unit along with a female escort officer.

Snake Eyes was extremely curious as to who it was that popped his bail, and thought whomever it was would be outside waiting for him. He became even more confused when he realized no one came to pick him up and that he had to get on the county jail van instead.

For the entire 25 minute drive on the highway Snake Eyes asked himself who in the hell paid his high ass bail. When the van pulled up downtown in front of the court house, his thoughts were interrupted when he heard one of the escorting officer's voice.

"Alright now, here we go", the grey haired black man announced.

The officer opened the doors to the back of the van, allowing Snake Eyes and the rest of the inmates to climb out.

"Damn, that hard ass metal got my ass hurting like hell," an older inmate complained as he stepped out of the van walking funny.

Without saying one word, Snake Eyes exited the van and began speed walking down the street, trying to get away from the correctional officers as quick as he could just in case they made a mistake and let him go. The last thing he was going to let happen was a re-arrest. Just then, the idea of his two young soldiers getting someone to pay his bail with the money they got away with from the bank robbery popped in his mind.

"Yeah yeah, it had to be them. They probably right at the hideout around this time too," he mumbled before jogging down the long street and around the corner.

There was no one outside on the street Snake Eyes was running down. He cut through the cemetery for a shortcut. He made it to the white and brown 2 story house and ran up the porch steps.

Snake Eyes balled his fist up and began banging on the door. BOOM! BOOM! BOOM! Within seconds, a male voice shouted from behind the door.
"Who is it!"

Snake Eyes recognized the voice and smiled slyly. *I knew they wasss going to be here*, he thought.
"It'ssss Sssnake Eyesss."

He heard the door unlock and the door knob twist before it finally opened. His young soldier appeared in the doorway with a surprised look on his face. "What'sss good yo, why the hell y'all ain't come to the jail and pick me up after y'all paid my bail?!" Snake Eyes hissed excitedly.

His little homie stepped to the side as Snake Eyes made his way in the house. The little homie he had ruffed up in the projects was sitting on the steps rolling up a fat blunt of weed. *How the hell this fuck boy get out of jail,* the young soldier thought as he continued to roll the blunt.

"We didn't pay your bail bro, we've been laying low ever since you got bumped off", the other soldier told him while shutting the door.

An extremely puzzled look appeared on Snake Eye's skinny face as he stood there speechless. *This piss head either told on somebody to get out, or had some money stashed away and popped his own bail and is really trying to be on some sarcastic shit,* the little homie with the weed thought. *That's alright though, I got a trick for his ass. I'm about to go grab my strap and let his bitch ass have it for that shit he did to me in the projects in front of everybody.*

The young boy stood up and looked at Snake Eyes. "A yo Snake Eyes, spark this blunt up for me big bro. I'm about to grab your share of the money from out the spot across the street real quick."

He stepped to Snake Eyes, handed him the blunt, and rushed towards the door. The other young boy looked at his partner type sideways because he knew it wasn't no money at the spot across the street.

As soon as the young boy reached for the door knob, a loud DOOM echoed throughout the house. The front door violently swung open, crashing against the young boy's head sending him flying to the floor. Real and Wild Sal rushed through the front door with their black semi automatic hand guns drawn. BLOW! BLOW! BLOW! BLOW! BLOW! Wild Sal let off several shots, striking the young boy in the torso sending him flying backwards into the couch.

Real rushed towards Snake Eyes growling like a vicious pit bull in pure rage before smacking him using all his might in the bridge of his nose with the butt of his black .45 caliber handgun. "Ugghhh!" Snake Eyes grunted.

He felt his nose bone crack and was in excruciating pain. His vision became blurry as the blood poured profusely down his face. Snake Eyes stumbled backwards and fell wildly over the couch. Real darted around the couch, looked down and noticed Snake Eyes on his knees, struggling to use his hands to get up from off the floor.
"Get up you bitch ass nigga!"

Real cocked his right leg back and kicked Snake Eyes in the ribs as hard as he could, cracking his frail ribs. Snake Eyes yelled in agony and started coughing up thick globs of blood. He curled up on the floor.

"That skinny muhfucka look like he sick or something, don't let his blood get on you," Wild Sal warned as he closed the front door, watching Real take all of his pinned up anger out on hopeless Snake Eyes.

Real was in a state of blind rage, he didn't even hear Sal warning him. With an extremely crazed look in his eyes, Real lifted his black hood up and tucked his pistol in between his waist and jeans.

"Don't curl up and put your tail in your ass now!" Real shouted like a maniac.

He leaned down and snatched Snake Eyes, who was still in pain gasping for air, up by his bloody white t-shirt aggressively then threw him forcefully against the speakers and stereo equipment, loudly knocking everything over and shattering a glass table.

"Ughh! Shit man!" Snake Eyes mumbled in pain.

Snake Eyes was too hurt to move so he just laid there with his body aching and bleeding all over the place.

Real wanted Snake Eyes so bad that he decided to post his bail, mirroring the same tactic Snake Eyes used on him when he shot Real with the shotgun. After all this time, Real finally got the opportunity to seek revenge on his worst enemy. It felt good. A sense of relief came over Real, making him feel like he was on top of the world.

Real started picking up speakers and slamming them on Snake Eyes.

"You see what happens when you fuck with me muhfucka!

Real finally picked up the last speaker and slammed it on Snake Eyes' back.
"Alright that's enough. You fuck around and kill him before we get to do what we planned," Wild Sal intervened.

Real still continued to stomp Snake Eyes. Sal rushed toward Real and quickly pulled him off of him.
"Chill out!"

Sal held Real back looking him in the eye. Once Real calmed down, Wild Sal turned around, pulled a thick rope out of his book bag, and proceeded to hog tie Snake Eyes. Wild Sal easily picked Snake Eyes frail frame up by his arms and began carrying him to the front door.

"Hurry up and go pop the trunk!"

Real was still breathing heavy. He hurriedly opened the front door and rushed towards the black intrepid parked a few feet away from the house. The creepy sound of huge rats squirming and squeaking echoed lightly through the air. The trunk of the car was filled with black and brown rats.

"Oh shit!"

Real jumped back when two of the rats jumped out of the trunk and scattered down the street. Seeing what happened, Wild Sal chuckled as he approached the trunk. He tossed Snake Eyes in and quickly closed it. Feeling the huge rats hungrily biting all over his bloody body, Snake Eyes awakened instantly. "Agghh!"

Snake Eyes cried out as loud as he could, trying to see through the pitch black darkness. He began moving around wildly. Wild Sal and Real climbed into the car and drove off.

chapter
Forty five minutes later, after driving down a long dark and empty road surrounded by an enormous field filled with huge trees, Wild Sal decided to turn down a barely visible dirt trail that led deep into the woods. For the last twenty minutes Snake Eyes had ben banging and kicking inside the trunk sill moaning from all the pain. *How the hell did he brake loose from the*

rope, Sal and Real wondered. After a while they came up with the conclusion that the rats must have chewed through the ropes.

Once Sal felt he was far enough, he pulled over and put the car in park, knowing no one would come this deep in to the woods this time of night. He left the lights on.

"Those rats tearing his ass up", Wild Sal said.

"Hand me my sword from the backseat," Real said calmly with a look of pure evil in his bloodshot eyes.

Wild Sal wanted to chuckle but he didn't, knowing this was an act of revenge that was very important and therapeutic to Real. He turned and grabbed the long sword from the backseat. It was tucked inside a black sheath. Real removed the cover, revealing the shiny long sharp 36 inch metal sword.

Wild Sal climbed out the vehicle, Real did too and strolled to the back of the car. Sal laughed silently at the sound of Snake Eyes screaming his head off. Real stood a few feet away clutching his sword tightly, positioning himself as if he was about to swing a baseball bat. Sal popped the trunk open and quickly took several steps back. Snake Eyes immediately climbed out of the trunk, screaming as loud as he could along with a crew of rats that clung to his body viciously chewing away at his back, chest, and head. He fell to the ground and began rolling around wildly trying to shake them off. He could barely see because one of the rates chewed his right eye out. His ears were also chewed off along with his lips and several fingers.

As soon as Snake Eyes got up on his feet and tried to make a run for it, Real ran up from behind and swung his sword, swiftly striking him in his leg. A sharp pain sprouted up Snake Eyes' leg and the crimson blood began pouring out of his open wound as he fell to the ground on his knees and hand like a sleezy whore preparing to get hit from the back.

"Time to die muhfucka!" Real growled with clinched teeth.

He stood over top of Snake Eyes, raised his bloody sword as high as his arms allowed, and violently hacked Snake Eyes in the back of his skinny neck like he had an ax in his hand chopping a huge chunk of wood. Snake Eyes gasped and his eyes grew wide. His body got stiff. The sharp blade only went half way through his neck so Real quickly raised his sword again and took another powerful hack, this time cutting his head off completely. Globs of blood poured from what was left on his neck as his body twitched.

Wild Sal cringed at the gruesome sight and quickly glanced away. The adrenaline still rushed through Real who just stood there with the sword in his hand breathing heavily, enjoying his moment of glory. He then turned around and looked at Wild Sal.

"Grab the shovels out the car so we can bury this piece of shit."

Sal grabbed two shovel's from the backseat and handed one of them to Real.

"We gonna dig the hole right over here", Real said firmly as he stepped over Snake Eyes' body.

The spot was near a huge tree. Real dug his shovel in the ground, scooped up dirt, and tossed it to the side. Wild Sal joined him. Real and Wild Sal dug a deep hole in the ground, tossed Snake Eyes' body in, and filled it back up with dirt.

After the hard labor, an exhausted Real picked Snake Eyes head up, cut his tongue out and picked up one of the dead rats on the ground and stuffed it in his mouth. Without saying a word he turned around and made his way to the car and got in the passenger side. Wild Sal checked to make sure they didn't leave any traces of evidence behind before jumping in the car and pulling off. The two were heading straight to Real's domain, the Dolly Holmes projects.

Real and Wild Sal arrived in the center of the projects. They pulled in front of the eight foot tall spiked black gate. Sal quickly turned the car lights off.

"You see anybody out here?" Real asked.

"Nah, I don't see nobody", Wild Sal replied after looking around thoroughly.

The entire projects was a ghost town. Real turned around in the seat, grabbed Snake Eyes' head out of the book bag and then got out of the car. He walked up to the black gate and placed the head on one of the spikes. Real got back in the car with Wild Sal and pulled off like nothing ever happened.

Real knew exactly what he was doing by leaving Snake Eyes hanging on the gate in the middle of the projects. He wanted everyone to wake up in the morning and see the fate of the man who humiliated and betrayed him deeply, who conquered his projects and ruled them viciously. Leaving a clear image of the heinous results if someone was to ever try such a thing again.

It was bright and early, around 7 a.m., when two crack addicts strolling through the projects spotted Snake Eyes' head on the gate. They were spooked the fuck out and ran off and told everyone they came in to contact with. Before you knew it, there were cops on the scene trying to investigate. Several crowds of people stood around staring in awe and disbelief at the gruesome image of Snake Eyes' head spiked on the gate. Some people were clueless as to what could have happened, but there was a fair amount of people from around the way that had a pretty good idea who was behind the abnormally horrific act. By the time the day was over the whole city was shook up like crazy, and everyone who was deep into the streets couldn't help but think to themselves...IT MUST HAVE BEEN REAL!

Coming Soon!

New Books Coming Soon:

Cold World 3
Diamond in the Dirt 5
Color Blind
Teflon Divas
Scarlow: Return of the Black Don
Venom in My Veins: The Untold Story of Snake Eyes

Books Available Now:

Cold World 1 & 2

Diamond in the Dirt 1 & 2 & 3

DIAMOND IN THE DIRT 4